ANNIE
AND THE
OLD ONE

ANNIE
AND THE
OLD ONE

by Miska Miles

Illustrated by Peter Parnall

Little, Brown and Company

Boston   Toronto   London

LIBRARY OF CONGRESS CATALOG CARD NO. 79-129900

ISBN 0-316-57117-2 (HC)

ISBN 0-316-57120-2 (PB)

HC: 20 19 18 17 16 15 14
PB: 20 19 18 17

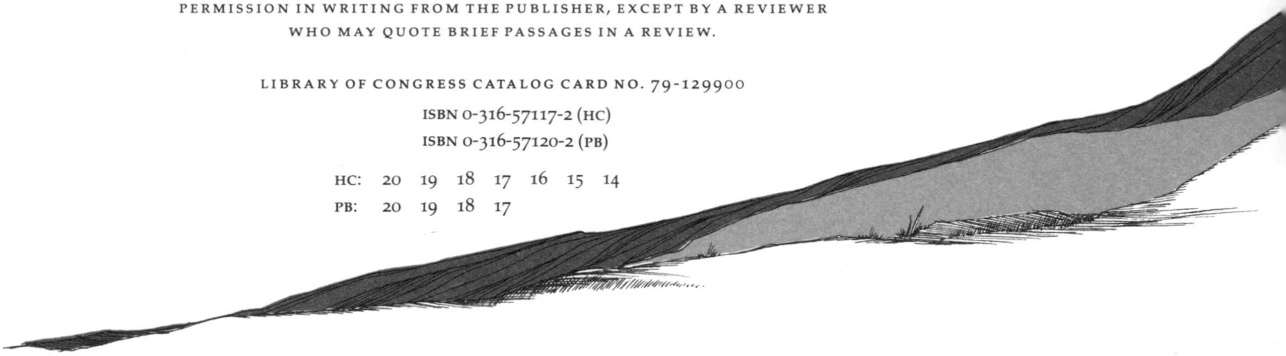

*Joy Street Books are published
by Little, Brown and Company (Inc.)*

AHS

*Published simultaneously in Canada
by Little, Brown & Company (Canada) Limited*

PRINTED IN THE UNITED STATES OF AMERICA

ANNIE
AND THE
OLD ONE

Annie's Navajo world was good—a world of rippling sand, of high copper-red bluffs in the distance, of the low mesa near her own snug hogan. The pumpkins were yellow in the cornfield, and the tassels on the corn were turning brown.

Each morning, the gate to the night pen near the hogan was opened wide and the sheep were herded to pasture on the desert.

Annie helped watch the sheep. She carried pails of water to the cornfield. And every weekday, she walked to the bus stop and waited for the yellow bus that took her to school and brought her home again.

Best of all were the evenings when she sat at her grandmother's feet and listened to stories of times long gone.

Sometimes it seemed to Annie that her grandmother was her age—a girl who had seen no more than nine or ten harvestings.

If a mouse skittered and jerked across the hard dirt floor of their hogan, Annie and her grandmother laughed together.

And when they prepared the fried bread for the evening meal, if it burned a bit black at the edges, they laughed and said it was good.

There were other times when her grandmother sat small and still, and Annie knew that she was very old. Then Annie would cover the thin knees of the Old One with a warm blanket.

It was at such a time that her grandmother said, "It is time you learn to weave, my granddaughter."

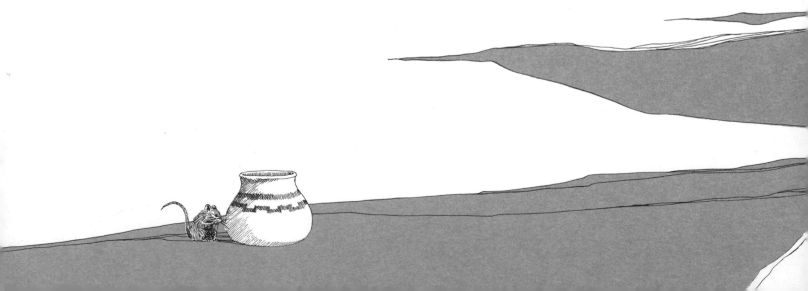

8

Annie touched the web of wrinkles that crisscrossed her grandmother's face and slowly went outside the hogan.

Beside the door, her father sat cross-legged, working with silver and fire, making a handsome, heavy necklace. Annie passed him and went to the big loom where her mother sat weaving.

Annie sat beside the loom, watching, while her mother slid the weaving stick in place among the strings of the warp. With red wool, her mother added a row to a slanting arrow of red, bright against the dull background.

Annie's thoughts wandered. She thought about the stories her grandmother had told—stories of hardship when rains flooded the desert—of dry weather when rains did not fall and the pumpkins and corn were dry in the field.

Annie looked out across the sand where the cactus bore its red fruit, and thought about the coyote—God's Dog—guarding the scattered hogans of the Navajos.

Annie watched while her mother worked. She made herself sit very still.

After a time, her mother looked at her and smiled. "Are you ready to weave, my daughter?"

Annie shook her head.

She continued to watch while her mother twisted the weaving stick in the warp, making a shed for the strands of gray and red wool.

At last her mother said softly, "You may go," almost as though she knew what Annie wanted.

Annie ran off to find her grandmother, and together they gathered twigs and brush to feed the small fire in the middle of the hogan.

When the evening meal was done, the old grandmother called her family together.

Annie and her mother and father stood quietly, respectfully, waiting for the grandmother to speak.

A coyote called shrilly from the mesa.

There was no sound in the hogan. There was no sound at all, except a small snap of the dying fire.

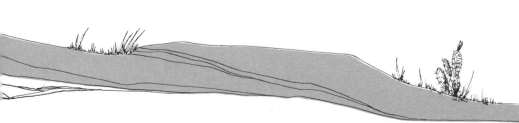

Then the grandmother spoke softly.

"My children, when the new rug is taken from the loom, I will go to Mother Earth."

Annie shivered and looked at her mother.

Her mother's eyes were shining bright with tears that did not fall, and Annie knew what her grandmother meant. Her heart stood still and she made no sound.

The Old One spoke again.

"You will each choose the gift that you wish to have."

Annie looked at the hard earth, swept smooth and clean.

"What will you have, my granddaughter?" the grandmother asked.

Annie looked at a weaving stick propped against the wall of the hogan. This was the grandmother's own weaving stick, polished and beautiful with age. Annie looked directly at the stick.

As though Annie had spoken, her grandmother nodded.

"My granddaughter shall have my weaving stick."

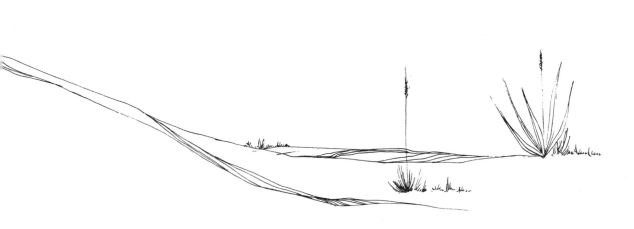

On the floor of the hogan lay a rug that the Old One had woven long, long ago. Its colors were mellowed and its warp and weft were strong.

Annie's mother chose the rug.

Annie's father chose the silver belt studded with turquoise that was now loose around the small waist of the Old One.

Annie folded her arms tightly across her stomach and went outside, and her mother followed.

"How can my grandmother know she will go to Mother Earth when the rug is taken from the loom?" Annie asked.

"Many of the Old Ones know," her mother said.

"How do they know?"

"Your grandmother is one of those who live in harmony with all nature—with earth, coyote, birds in the sky. They know more than many will ever learn. Those Old Ones know." Her mother sighed deeply. "We will speak of other things."

In the days that followed, the grandmother went about her work much as she had always done.

She ground corn to make meal for bread.

She gathered dry twigs and brush to make fire.

And when there was no school, she and Annie watched the sheep and listened to the sweet, clear music of the bell on the collar of the lead goat.

The weaving of the rug was high on the loom. It was almost as high as Annie's waist.

"My mother," Annie said, "why do you weave?"

"I weave so we may sell the rug and buy the things we must have from the trading post. Silver for silvermaking. Deer hide for boots—"

"But you know what my grandmother said—"

Annie's mother did not speak. She slid her weaving stick through the warp and picked up a strand of rose-red wool.

Annie turned and ran. She ran across the sand and huddled in the shallow shade of the small mesa. Her grandmother would go back to the earth when the rug was taken from the loom. The rug must not be finished. Her mother must not weave.

The next morning, where her grandmother went, Annie followed.

When it was time to go to the bus stop to meet the school bus, she dawdled, walking slowly and watching her feet. Perhaps she would miss the bus.

And then quite suddenly she did not want to miss it. She knew what she must do.

She ran hard, as fast as she could—breathing deeply—and the yellow bus was waiting for her at the stop.

She climbed aboard. The bus moved on, stopping now and then at hogans along the way. Annie sat there alone and made her plan.

In school, she would be bad, so bad that the teacher would send for her mother and father.

And if her mother and father came to school to talk to the teacher, that would be one day when her mother could not weave. One day.

On the playground, Annie's teacher was in charge of the girls' gymnasium class.

"Who will lead the exercises today?" the teacher asked.

No one answered.

The teacher laughed. "Very well. Then I shall be leader." The teacher was young, with yellow hair. Her blue skirt was wide and the heels on her brown shoes were high. The teacher kicked off her shoes and the girls laughed.

Annie followed the teacher's lead—bending, jumping, and she

waited for the time when the teacher would lead them in jogging around the playground.

As Annie jogged past the spot where the teacher's shoes lay on the ground, she picked up a shoe and hid it in the folds of her dress.

And when Annie jogged past a trash can, she dropped the shoe inside.

Some of the girls saw her and laughed, but some frowned and were solemn.

When the line jogged near the schoolhouse door, Annie slipped from the line and went inside to her room and her own desk.

Clearly she heard the teacher as she spoke to the girls outside.

"The other shoe, please." Her voice was pleasant. There was silence.

Limping, one shoe on and one shoe gone, the teacher came into the room.

The girls followed, giggling and holding their hands across their mouths.

"I know it's funny," the teacher said, "but now I need the shoe."

Annie looked at the boards of the floor. A shiny black beetle crawled between the cracks.

The door opened and a man teacher came inside with a shoe in

his hand. As he passed Annie's desk, he touched her shoulder and smiled down at her.

"I saw someone playing tricks," he said.

The teacher looked at Annie and the room was very still.

When school was over for the day, Annie waited.

Timidly, with hammering heart, she went to the teacher's desk.

"Do you want my mother and father to come to the school to-morrow?" she asked.

"No, Annie," the teacher said. "I have the shoe. Everything is all right."

Annie's face was hot and her hands were cold. She turned and ran. She was the last to climb on the bus.

Finally, there was her own bus stop. She hopped down and slowly trudged the long way home. She stopped beside the loom.

The rug was now much higher than her waist.

25

That night she curled up in her blanket. She slept lightly, and awakened before dawn.

There was no sound from her mother's sheepskin. Her grandmother was a quiet hump in her blanket. Annie heard only her father's loud, sleeping breathing. There was no other sound on the whole earth, except the howling of a coyote from far across the desert.

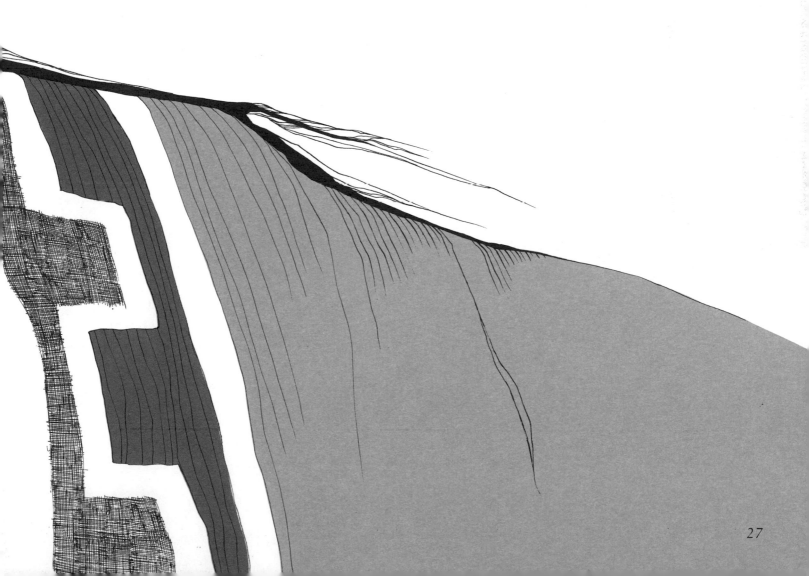

In the dim light of early morning, Annie crept outside to the night pen where the sheep were sleeping.

The dry wood creaked when she opened the gate and pushed it wide open against the fence.

She tugged at the sleeping sheep until one stood quietly. Then the others stood also, uncertain — shoving together. The lead goat turned toward the open gate and Annie slipped her fingers through his belled collar. She curled her fingertips across the bell, muffling its sound, and led the goat through the gate. The sheep followed.

She led them across the sand and around the small mesa where she released the goat.

"Go," she said.

She ran back to the hogan, and slithered under her blanket and lay shivering. Now her family would hunt the sheep all day. This would be a day when her mother would not weave.

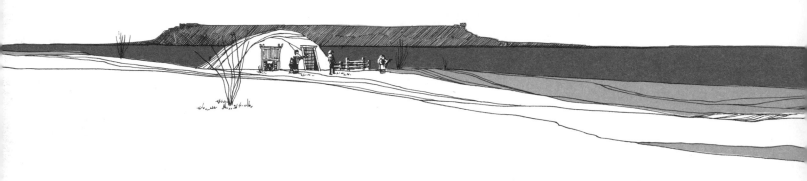

When the fullness of morning came and it was light, Annie
watched her grandmother rise and go outside.

Annie heard her call.

"The sheep are gone."

Annie's mother and father hurried outside and Annie followed.

Her mother moaned softly, "The sheep — the sheep —"

"I see them," the grandmother said. "They graze near the
mesa."

Annie went with her grandmother and when they reached the
sheep, Annie's fingers slipped under the goat's collar and the bell
tingled sharply as the sheep followed back to the pen.

In school that day, Annie sat quietly and wondered what more she could do. When the teacher asked questions, Annie looked at the floor. She did not even hear.

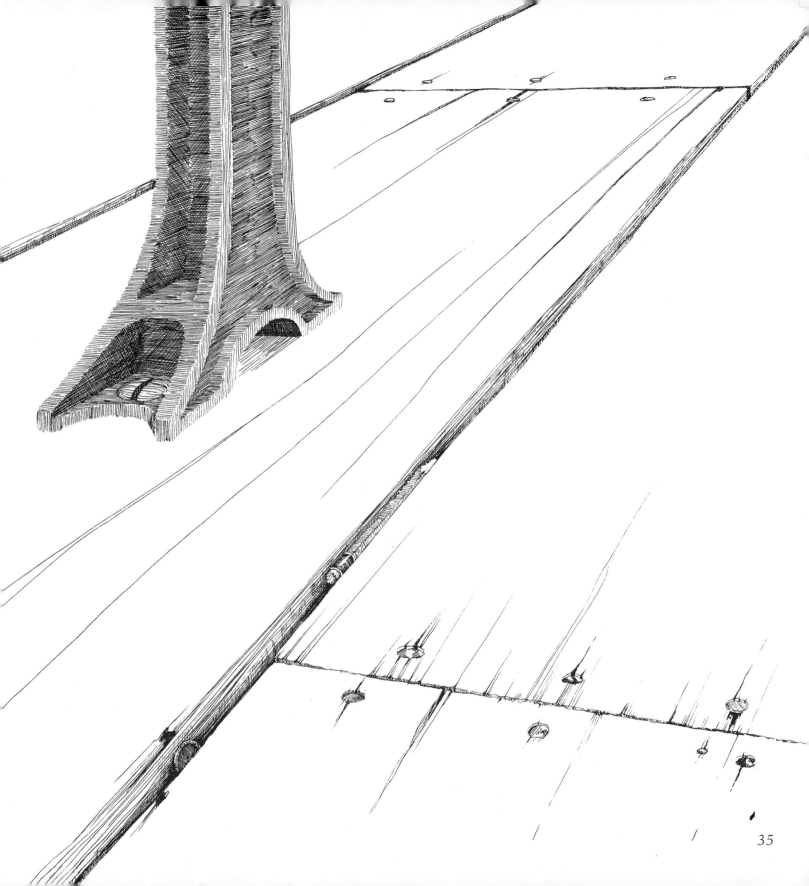

When night came, she curled up in her blanket, but not to sleep.

When everything was still, she slipped from her blanket and crept outside.

The sky was dark and secret. The wind was soft against her face. For a moment she stood waiting until she could see in the night. She went to the loom.

She felt for the weaving stick there in its place among the warp strings. She separated the warp and felt for the wool.

Slowly she pulled out the strands of yarn, one by one.

One by one, she laid them across her knees.

And when the row was removed, she separated the strings of the warp again, and reached for the second row.

When the woven rug was only as high as her waist, she crept back to her blanket, taking the strands of wool with her.

Under her blanket, she smoothed the strands and made them into a ball. And then she slept.

The next night, Annie removed another day's weaving.

In the morning when her mother went to the loom, she looked at the weaving—puzzled—

For a moment, she pressed her fingers against her eyes.

The Old One looked at Annie curiously. Annie held her breath.

The third night, Annie crept to the loom.

A gentle hand touched her shoulder.

"Go to sleep, my granddaughter," the Old One said.

Annie wanted to throw her arms around her grandmother's waist and tell her why she had been bad, but she could only stumble to her blanket and huddle under it and let the tears roll into the edge of her hair.

When morning came, Annie unrolled herself from the blanket and helped prepare the morning meal.

Afterward, she followed her grandmother through the cornfield. Her grandmother walked slowly, and Annie fitted her steps to the slow steps of the Old One.

When they reached the small mesa, the Old One sat crossing her knees, folding her gnarled fingers into her lap.

Annie knelt beside her.

The Old One looked far off toward the rim of desert where sky met sand.

"My granddaughter," she said, "you have tried to hold back time. This cannot be done." The desert stretched yellow and brown away to the edge of the morning sky. "The sun comes up from the edge of earth in the morning. It returns to the edge of earth in the evening. Earth, from which good things come for the living creatures on it. Earth, to which all creatures finally go."

Annie picked up a handful of brown sand and pressed it against the palm of her hand. Slowly, she let it fall to earth. She understood many things.

The sun rose but it also set.

The cactus did not bloom forever. Petals dried and fell to earth.

She knew that she was a part of the earth and the things on it. She would always be a part of the earth, just as her grandmother had always been, just as her grandmother would always be, always and forever.

And Annie was breathless with the wonder of it.

They walked back to the hogan together, Annie and the Old One.

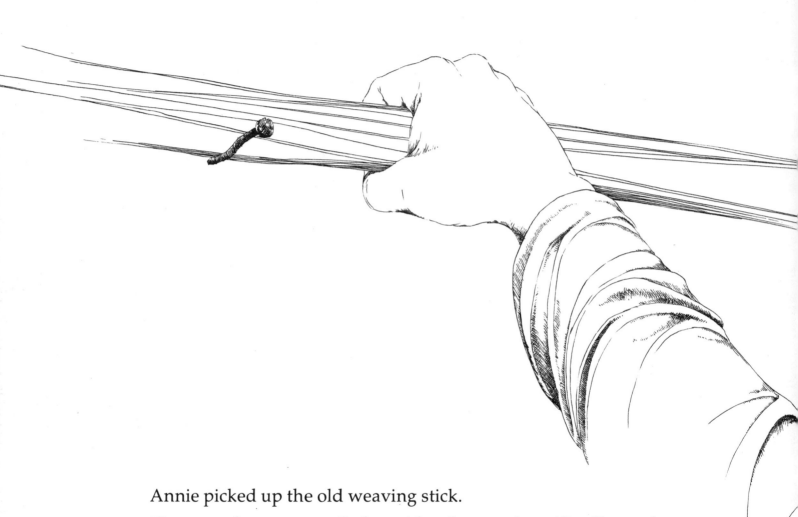

Annie picked up the old weaving stick.

"I am ready to weave," she said to her mother. "I will use the stick that my grandmother has given me." She knelt at the loom.

She separated the warp strings and slipped the weaving stick in place, as her mother had done, as her grandmother had done.

She picked up a strand of gray wool and started to weave.